Mariella Mystery

Investigates

A Cupcake conundrum

Mariella Mystery

Investigates

A Cupcake Conundrum

by
Kate Pankhurst

BARRON'S

First edition for the United States published in 2014
by Barron's Educational Series, Inc.

First published in Great Britain in 2013
by Orion Children's Books, a division of the Orion Publishing
Group Ltd., Orion House, 5 Upper St. Martin's Lane,
London WC2H 9EA Great Britain

All inquiries should be addressed to:
Barron's Educational Series, Inc.
250 Wireless Boulevard, Hauppauge, New York 11788
www.barronseduc.com

ISBN: 978-1-4380-0459-4

Library of Congress Control No. 2013949192

Manufactured by M17P17L, York, PA

Date of Manufacture: June 2014

Printed in the United States of America

9 8 7 6 5 4 3 2 1

For Mum: enjoy the cakes ...

me ↑ (cake — YUM!)

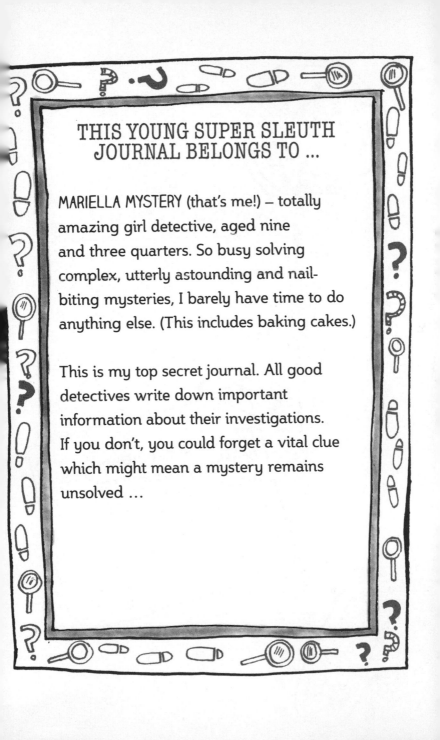

THIS YOUNG SUPER SLEUTH JOURNAL BELONGS TO ...

MARIELLA MYSTERY (that's me!) – totally amazing girl detective, aged nine and three quarters. So busy solving complex, utterly astounding and nail-biting mysteries, I barely have time to do anything else. (This includes baking cakes.)

This is my top secret journal. All good detectives write down important information about their investigations. If you don't, you could forget a vital clue which might mean a mystery remains unsolved ...

(If you are my annoying brother, Arthur, STEP AWAY. This book will self-destruct in five, four, three, two ...)

Apron

Saturday May 3rd

The mystery Girls

taking a break from mystery solving

(tree house)

HQ

3:00 PM
MYSTERY GIRLS HQ

Even when I'm not solving mysteries I can still use my amazing detective skills to help other people. Today the Mystery Girls completed an important mission. This is my mission report in full:

OPERATION BAKE-A-CAKE

PRIMARY OBJECTIVE: To make sure fellow Mystery Girl and BRILLIANT baker, Violet Maple, gets through to the finals of her favorite TV program — Bake or Break.

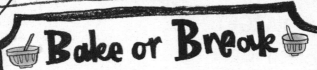

Bake or Break

AUDITION FOR BAKE OR BREAK, THE JUNIOR COMPETITION!

Do you have what it takes to become the nation's best junior baker?

If you can't stand the heat, get out of the kitchen. If you can, get in it and show us what you and your cakes, pies, and pastries are made of!

Bake or Break – the baking competition where you'll bake – or break!

(WARNING: Common side effects of "breaking" include nervousness, hysteria, and uncontrollable sobbing. Contestants enter at their own risk.)

(I haven't seen it before but Violet says it's really difficult and if you win you are officially the best young baker in the whole country.)

THE TARGET:
Violet Maple

Totally amazing girl detective (like me!) with the ability to bake the tastiest cakes ever. Has been known to have "Maple Meltdowns" while mystery solving. We don't want that to happen at Bake or Break.

Violet

Totally AMAZING CAKES made by Violet

blue tart ↓ (unusual)

sparkle buns

eight layer chocolate fizz cake

mystery whirls

POPPY in her swimming cap

Poppy Holmes

Mystery Girl with a passion for finding clues and synchronized swimming.

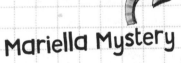

Mariella Mystery

(Me) Brilliantly talented at detective work. Big fan of cakes baked by Violet, and most other types of cake.

me

NOTE: Failure is not an option. This has been Violet's ambition since she was five, when she first baked a cake with her Grandma Maple.

8:45 AM: Leaving Mystery Girls HQ, Operation Bake-a-Cake is intercepted by the Prince of Annoyingness, Arthur Mystery (claims to be my little brother). He is waving his Bake or

Arthur (annoying)

Break Annual book and begs us to tell Bake or Break he is seven, not five and a half, so he can enter too. I say no way.

8:55 AM: Bake or Break auditions, Puddleford Village Hall. The only way Poppy and I could gain access to the auditions was to enter the competition ourselves.
I don't know much about baking, but I know I like cake.

mmm, cake!

14

9:03 AM: Violet has laid out her ingredients and is busy reading Grandma Maple's recipe book. It's full of useful baking information and has helped Violet think up loads of great ideas for her own recipes (with a mysterious twist).

9:05 AM: Poppy and I find tables next to Violet where we can watch for signs of stress. If we spot them early, hopefully we can avoid a full scale Maple Meltdown.

A maple meltdown

A DELICIOUS SLICE OF RAINBOW CAKE

RECIPE: you will need

9:15 AM: I get out my recipe for Rainbow Cake. I've never tried baking anything before, but I don't think it will be difficult — not compared to mystery-solving.

9:30 AM: The Bake or Break Talent Spotter says we all need to take this really seriously — if we bake some wonderful cakes we could go through to the next audition and even to the finals on TV. She says, "This is Bake or Break, guys. Five ... four ... three ... two ... one ... BAKE!"

9:45 AM: Violet is staring into space holding a mixing bowl and a whisk. I alert Poppy using our emergency code word: FLAPJACK. We bang pots and pans. Violet snaps out of her trance and leaps into action. Meltdown averted.

10:30 AM: Poppy takes her cake out of the oven. It makes a weird fizzing noise and then explodes. Poppy deduces the twelve bags of popping candy she put in gave her cake too much "pop." My cake doesn't look like the picture in the recipe either.

11:00 AM: TENSE MOMENT. We hear Violet say, "I'm not sure about this" worriedly to herself. This is a clear sign she is starting to panic. (She is icing her Mystery Cake.) Poppy runs over and fans Violet with a towel.

11:30 AM: The Talent Spotter shouts that our time is up and judging of the cakes (the ones that survived baking) will commence. She tastes my cake first and looks as if she might throw up. (I deduce that I'm definitely better at being a detective than baking.)

11:32 AM: The Bake or Break talent spotter said Violet's cake showed star potential! WOW. The mysterious part of her Mystery Cake was revealed when you cut into it. Inside there was a different colored piece of cake in the shape of a question mark.

11:35 AM: Operation Bake-a-Cake is a success! Violet is through to the next audition! She is definitely going to win the competition and write a best-selling recipe book all about mysterious cakes. It could have recipes in it like the Truffles of Doom, or the Disappearing Cupcake, or something like that. I feel so proud of her.

PART ONE OF MISSION: COMPLETE!

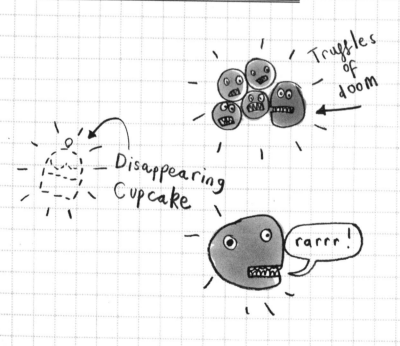

Tuesday
May 6th

mmmm

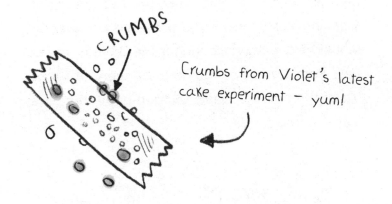

CRUMBS

Crumbs from Violet's latest
cake experiment — yum!

cake

6:30 PM
MYSTERY GIRLS HQ

Violet had the day off from school today to go to the next round of auditions and she was just here with some AMAZING NEWS! She is through to the finals of Bake or Break, on actual TV! And extra amazingness – the TV company has chosen our school field as the location for the Bake or Break tent! Poppy and I are going to be there to support Violet through the whole thing. (I hope there are loads of free cake.)

So, instead of Mystery Girl team meetings, Poppy
says we need to cover every aspect of Coping
at an Extreme Baking Competition in Intensive
Preparation Sessions.

Tonight we've been recreating conditions Violet
might experience in the Bake or Break kitchens.
I created extreme heat by blasting hot air into
HQ from Mom's travel blow dryer and Poppy
banged some pans together to represent distracting
"sounds of the kitchen." Violet coped really well in
Mystery Girls HQ but she's still worried about what
it will actually be like in the competition.

Violet worries about stuff all the time. It's our job to make sure she keeps calm. (I've had loads of practice at this – detectives need to be calm and level-headed in all sorts of tricky situations.)

"I feel so nervous," said Violet. "What if my baking is terrible compared to the other contestants?"

"They might be talented, but I'm sure none of them will have the same mysterious edge as you," I said. (Auditions have been held all around the country so we won't know who the other four contestants are until the competition starts next week, but I'm sure this is true.)

Violet learned to bake with her Grandma Maple. Grandma Maple is really well known in Puddleford as the only person to ever win the Puddleford Summer Festival's "Best Bake in Show" award ten years in a row.

Grandma Maple

TASTY
creamy
gooey
THE MAPLE MARVEL

One of her recipes, the Maple Marvel, became famous after it received the highest score EVER. Lots of people asked Grandma Maple for the recipe but she said it was absolutely top secret.

Grandma Maple is away at the moment on a cooking cruise, tasting cakes from other countries. She mailed her recipe book to Violet, saying she hoped it would bring her luck in the competition. It definitely has so far!

grandma maple

Violet has come up with loads of cake ideas that she's been adding to the recipe book for Grandma Maple to read when she gets back.

"Just remember Grandma Maple's advice," I said to Violet. (Grandma Maple has written lots of good baking advice in the recipe book.) "Keep calm and concentrate on the cakes!" That's my favorite one.

Ice **E**xplosion **B**un

FROZEN cherry

ice cream center

raspberry ripple sponge

Abominable Snowman Cake

sweets

mysterious

Violet's cake idea

Friday
May 9th

Some varieties of cake

victoria sponge

butterfly cake

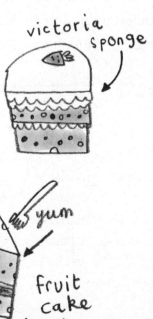

yum

fruit cake

5:30 PM
MYSTERY GIRLS HQ (2 DAYS UNTIL THE BAKE OR BREAK FINALS START!)

We've been watching past shows of Bake or Break after school and I'm starting to see why Violet is so nervous. She is going to face four different baking challenges over four days, and they don't look easy.

1. THE CUPCAKE CHALLENGE:
Bake the most exciting and unique cupcake you possibly can. One past contestant actually managed to bake hovering cupcakes with little jet packs in them. That's just crazy.

2. THE PICNIC BASKET CHALLENGE: The judges pull a random type of picnic food from a picnic basket that the contestants must bake. In the episodes we watched, this was where loads of contestants experienced "breaking." One girl realized she'd forgotten the jelly layer in her trifle. Trying to block out the extreme embarrassment of the incident, she stuck her head in a bowl of whipped cream and refused to move. (It sounds funny but it was really serious — she almost suffocated!)

3. THE CHILDREN'S PARTY CHALLENGE: The judges will be looking for a really complicated birthday cake. If it's not exciting enough, contestants get cream pies thrown at them while they bake. Pressure!

4. THE SHOW-STOPPER CHALLENGE:

This is a chance for contestants to bake a cake that shows off their talents. Violet told us she is planning a new take on the award-winning and famous Maple Marvel cake (with a secret and mysterious edge).

"How am I going to find time to practice making my Show-Stopper recipe on top of everything else?" said Violet, biting her fingernails.

"Relax," said Poppy. "The Show-Stopper Challenge is the last in the competition – you've got a lot of time."

"But what if the judges hate it? What if they think I can't bake? What if … what if …"

"Violet, pull yourself together. The judges are going to love you," said Poppy, shooting me a worried look.

I know why Poppy is worried. After watching Bake or Break, I've realized the judges are tough – very tough.

HARRIET BLYTHINGTON: Has been a Bake or Break judge for years and years. She's hard to please and is famous around the world for her meringue-whipping. She insists on whisking by hand and thinks electric mixers are for wimps. One year she banned them from Bake or Break, but nearly all the contestants ended up "breaking" due to severe arm cramps. She is one of Violet's all-time baking heroes.

JUDGE HARRIET BLYTHINGTON

SPENCER SPOKES:
Famous for thinking of weird recipes you can cook using vegetables. He's only been a judge on Bake or Break for three years (the last one quit because of the extreme stress of the competition) but he's already well known for saying exactly what he thinks. He doesn't care that he is talking to kids. Mom's got his new recipe book *Parsnips and Me.* (A whole book about parsnips? Sounds BORING.)

SPENCE R SPOKES

It's up to me and Poppy to make sure Violet is ready to face them on Monday.

— BORING!

MONDAY
May 12th

BAKE OR BREAK FINALS,
DAY ONE:
THE CUPCAKE CHALLENGE

me

Cake!

(And it's Spring Vacation.
A whole week off
school — wohooooh!)

11:20 AM
BAKE OR BREAK TENT,
VIP AUDIENCE AREA

It's the first day of Bake or Break, and as Official
Team Violet Supporters, Poppy and I have
VIP passes. Arthur is totally jealous. He's started
carrying his Bake or Break Annual everywhere
and keeps saying being on Bake or Break is his
greatest ambition. That's only because he
overheard Violet saying it was hers. He'll do
anything to try and impress us because he wants
to be a Mystery Girl. (There's no
way that will ever happen.)

annoying!

BAKE or
BREAK
the annual

Our school field has been taken over by the huge Bake or Break tent. Inside, there are areas set up like mini kitchens with cookers and sinks and cabinets for the five finalists. I'm so excited Violet is one of them! We've got really good seats in the VIP audience area – close to the baking action.

mini kitchen area

"Violet looked really nervous, didn't she?" said Poppy.

"This competition is designed to break bakers, Poppy," I said. "But if those sherbet apple cupcakes she brought to HQ yesterday are anything to go by, she'll be fine."

Hang on – this is it, the contestants are about to come out!

12:00 PM
BAKE OR BREAK TENT – WE MEET
THE BAKERS!

Some moody music began to play and smoke
started to pour out of a doorway at the back
of the kitchen. (I think it was fake smoke to
make the kitchens look atmospheric, not from a
burned cake or anything.) A voice boomed into
the tent:

**"WELCOME TO THE BAKE OR BREAK
JUNIOR COMPETITION! PLEASE
GIVE A WARM WELCOME TO YOUR
JUDGES ... THE WORLD-FAMOUS
MISTRESS OF MERINGUE. HARRIET
BLYTHINGTON..."**

HARRIET

BIG
arm

Harriet emerged from the smoke and waved to the audience. Even in a floral pink apron, she looked scary.

"Wow, she really does have one arm that's a lot bigger than the other!" said Poppy. (Harriet has one really muscly arm from the years of intensive meringue-whipping.)

"And he's almost good enough to eat. He's passionate about parsnips. It's the delectable Spencer Spokes!"

Spencer strode out of the smoky doorway, wearing a T-shirt with a parsnip on it. He waved casually at the audience, and ran his fingers through his hair.

Dazzling Smile

"Now it's time to give a warm welcome to this year's Bake or Break contestants..." came the voice again. "Put your hands together for the Saviour of School Dinners, Marie Sloops!"

There was some coughing (there was a lot of fake smoke now) and a small girl with her hair in two braids walked out of the smoke grinning like this was the best thing to happen to her, ever. She took her place on one of five stools next to the judges.

"Next up, if you like glitter, you'll go crazy for the baking of our next finalist. It's the Princess of Cake Perfection, Primula Gordon!"

Primula leaped through the smoke with a huge smile on her face. She winked at the camera as she skipped to her stool.

She didn't even look at Marie, but just sat with her hands perched on her knees.

Her face looked like it must have been really hurting from smiling so much. Nobody can smile for that long and really mean it. It's a bit fake if you ask me.

"We are delighted to present Bake or Break Baking scientist, Oliver Pickett ..."

A small boy waved his way through the smoke. He readjusted his round glasses and walked to his stool. He looked like he would be more at home in a school library than a baking competition.

"The Icing on the Cake – that's how judges described our next young icing expert – it's Patsy Éclair!"

Patsy strutted out to the stools. She put her hand on her hip and flashed the audience a smile. This girl obviously isn't here to make friends – she means serious baking business.

"Baking talent runs in her family —
it's the grand-daughter of Puddleford's
most famous baker and
creator of the most
mysterious cakes in
town — Violet Maple!"

TOTALLY
going to win!

Wow, that was such a good
intro! It makes Violet sound
totally amazing.

Violet walked at top speed through the smoke
cloud, not looking at the audience. This wasn't
ideal. It sent a message that she might "break"
instead of bake.

Next up they were going to show the films made
at the contestants' houses. Violet said she was
going to be too nervous to listen properly to
useful information about the other contestants,
so I promised to gather as many facts as possible.

THE CONTESTANTS

MARIE SLOOPS: Daughter of a dinner lady. Selected for her new twist on school dinner favorites. When she grows up she wants to make sure all school dinners are as delicious as her mom's. (Violet will definitely win if Marie makes food like the school dinners we get!)

yuck

PRIMULA GORDON: Primula says all the cakes she makes are AMAZING. Also says she is the best at horse riding (has her own pony called Cupcake) and the best at dancing. (I have a strong suspicion Primula is a total show-off.)

show off pony

OLIVER PICKETT: Experiments with strange ingredients in his baking laboratory to make bizarre cakes like ketchup, chip and baked bean buns. Keeps all his recipes top secret, even from his mom and dad. Could have unexpected baking tricks Violet will need to watch out for.

PATSY ÉCLAIR: Film shows her kitchen full of amazingly decorated cakes. Patsy says, "Did I bake them? Oh, they are just something I whipped up earlier. I find baking so easy, you see — especially icing." (EXTREME SMUGNESS ALERT!)

VIOLET MAPLE: Film shows her reading Grandma Maple's recipe book and talking about the family recipes she likes to bake, especially the Maple Marvel. A raincoat and fedora hat isn't what you would usually wear to bake cakes in, but Violet explains she's wearing them because she is a Mystery Girl. (WOW, we got a mention!)

cool!

HANG ON! Did I just see Primula Gordon snicker? I hope she isn't laughing about Violet being a Mystery Girl. Must tell Violet to avoid her.

12:30 PM
BAKE OR BREAK TENT, KITCHEN AREA

When filming finished, the contestants started to set up their workspaces for the Cupcake Challenge. Violet looked as if she was panicking – opening cabinet doors and searching drawers.

I managed to distract Violet's mom and dad, pointing them in the direction of Spencer Spokes, who was signing books for a crowd of giggling moms. We needed Mystery Girl time alone with Violet to calm her down.

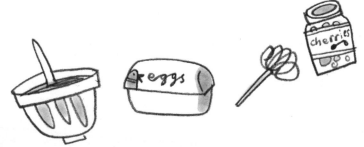

"This is going to be a disaster! I'm going to make a massive idiot of myself on TV!" Violet said, when we went over to her kitchen area.

"Violet, you could do the Cupcake Challenge with your eyes closed!" said Poppy.

"No! You don't understand, it's gone, I've lost it …" Violet said, clutching the worktop.

"Of course you haven't lost it, Violet. You've still got a talent for baking," I said.

This is BAD Look

"Mariella's right – don't break this early in the competition. Remember all the Intensive Preparation Sessions we've done," said Poppy. She gave me a look that said, "This is bad, very bad."

"But it's gone, I don't know how ... I promised I wouldn't ..." Violet said. She was getting hysterical.

"Pull yourself together, Violet!" I said, wondering if I should throw a glass of cold water over her.

shock

cold water

HOW TO CALM A HYSTERICAL PERSON

"THE BOOK! I've lost Grandma Maple's lucky recipe book!" Violet spluttered.

Uh oh. It was worse than we'd thought. The recipe book is really special to Violet. She believes it has brought her luck so far in the competition. And she'd promised Grandma Maple she'd look after it.

"Think back to where you last had it – what have you done since then?" I said.

"I was making some notes on my Cupcake Challenge recipe, then I left it on a table while the film crew interviewed me," said Violet. "I was talking about Grandma Maple and how she let me borrow her book because she thinks I'm good enough to follow in her footsteps. But when I came back the recipe book had gone!"

"Violet," I said, getting suspicious now, "Was anyone else nearby when you left the book?"

MISSING!

"The other contestants were getting ready to start filming," said Violet. "I asked them and they said they hadn't seen anyone move it."

"Violet, I don't think they would say they'd seen what had happened to the recipe book," I said. My mystery senses were tuned in.

"But why wouldn't they?" said Violet.

"You are too nice," said Poppy. Her mystery senses were tuned in too.

"I don't understand," said Violet, puzzled. (She must be very distracted by the pressures of Bake or Break, because she would usually have figured this out by now.)

"I suspect your book has been taken by someone, somebody trying to ruin your chances in the competition," I said.

NEW MYSTERY TO SOLVE: ~~THE CASE OF THE MISSING RECIPE BOOK~~ THE CUPCAKE CONUNDRUM* (Because that sounds loads more exciting than the Case of the Missing Recipe Book.)

*Conundrum: This is a really confusing and difficult problem or mystery. (Not too difficult for the Mystery Girls, though.)

1:20 PM
BAKE OR BREAK TENT, VIP CANTEEN AREA (LUNCHTIME)

I never expected to open a new case file today. It just goes to show that the Young Super Sleuth's Handbook was right. You never know when a mystery might present itself.

Even though Violet is really shaken up by the disappearance of the recipe book, she managed to give us a detailed statement about what had happened just before it vanished:

Turn over to read the victim's statements

VIOLET MAPLE: VICTIM'S STATEMENT

10:45 AM: Violet is in a backstage area where the contestants and judges get loads of free cake. Violet is too nervous to eat any, so she makes some notes in Grandma Maple's recipe book instead.

10:55 AM: Marie Sloops comes over and asks what Violet is reading. She says her mom said, when she's older she'll be given the Sloops' Family recipe book.

10:57 AM: Primula Gordon overhears and says that she doesn't need to read a recipe book because she is really good at inventing recipes, the best in the competition probably. (My suspicions were right; she is a total show-off.)

SHOW OFF!

cake expert

Recipes TOP secret

11:00 AM: Oliver Pickett asks them to be quiet because he is concentrating on working out a very complicated recipe.

11:07 AM: Violet tries to make conversation with Patsy Éclair and asks if she's feeling nervous. Patsy says she's pretty sure the challenges will be so easy that it will be no problem for her to win. (That girl is WAY too confident.)

11:15 AM: Violet feels really nervous now. When the film crew ask her to do a short interview she accidentally leaves Grandma Maple's recipe book on a table.

11:25 AM: Violet gets back from her interview and realizes the book is gone.

lost it

11:30 AM: Primula tells Violet she's probably just lost it or something. The Bake or Break crew say she'll have to stop looking because it's time to go on set and introduce herself.

The Young Super Sleuth's Handbook says that a good detective should be careful not to get carried away making a mystery more mysterious or dramatic than it really is. As far as I can see, there are two explanations for what has happened to Grandma Maple's recipe book.

More logical and less dramatic explanation: Violet has lost the book. She was so nervous about the competition that she didn't put it on the table, but accidentally threw it in the trash can or left it on a tray of cakes without realizing.

TRASH CAN

whoops

Also logical but much more dramatic explanation: Grandma Maple's recipe book was TAKEN. Whoever it was overheard Violet talking about what a famous baker Grandma Maple is and how Violet hopes to be as good as her. They don't want her to have a chance at winning – so they took the recipe book.

I put my logical explanations to Violet and she said she is absolutely sure she put the book on the table, not on a plate of cakes or in the trash can.

This means our suspicions are correct – somebody, a contestant, a judge, or a member of the crew has **stolen** Grandma Maple's recipe book.

WHAT TYPE OF MYSTERY ARE YOU SOLVING?

It isn't always clear at the start of an investigation what type of mystery you are trying to solve. There are four main types of mystery to look out for.

WHODUNITS? – This is when you need to get to the bottom of who has committed a crime or mysterious act.

WHYDUNITS? – You might know *who* was likely to have caused a mystery, but you don't know *why* they did it. You'll have to work hard to find a motive in this type of case.

WHATDUNUITS? – Something mysterious has happened. It may appear that it was not the work of a human being. Could you be dealing with animals, aliens, ghosts, or other supernatural creatures?

WHERE-IS-ITS? – When something has gone missing, you'll have to follow clues and trails to find it again.

2:15 PM
BAKE OR BREAK TENT –
CUPCAKE CHALLENGE BEGINS

When all the contestants came onto the set for the Cupcake Challenge this afternoon, the crowd cheered.

"Welcome to the Bake or Break junior competition!" Harriet Blythington said. "The standard this year is very high, but the challenges will be tough."

"Very tough," Spencer Spokes added, giving the audience a dramatic look.

Spencer's LOOK

"Cupcakes may look easy to bake, but they are deceptively difficult," Harriet continued.

"And this might be the junior
competition, but I don't want to
see sponges like breeze blocks
or icing that looks like it was
done by a nine-year-old."

(Harriet said it like she hadn't noticed that most of
the contestants were actually nine.)

"We'll be looking for creative flair.
The sort of baking you'd see in
my latest book. Did I mention my
latest book, *Parsnips and Me?*"
Spencer said.

Harriet rolled her eyes. "Contestants, you have
two hours to bake the most perfect cupcakes we
have ever seen. Three, two, one – BAKE!"

The most perfect cupcakes they've ever seen?
PRESSURE!

2:45 PM
BAKE OR BREAK TENT – SURVEILLANCE
OF CUPCAKE CHALLENGE CONTINUES ...

So far, Violet seems to be handling the pressure well. She said she doesn't want to disappoint Grandma Maple so she's going to give the challenge everything she's got. That means Poppy and I can focus on finding clues. We're looking out for anyone doing anything weird. Like secretly looking in Grandma Maple's recipe book for tips.

The Bake or Break cameras have been filming the contestants and showing the footage on the huge screen at the back of the kitchen.

Oliver Pickett doesn't like being filmed very much. There's something a bit weird about him. Why does he need to be so secretive?

"I can't possibly tell you how I'm going to make the explosive filling for my volcano cupcakes. It's a top-secret combination of carefully selected ingredients," said Oliver.

The cameras headed toward Marie Sloops who looked up and grinned, then Primula Gordon darted in front of her.

"I'm at a really important stage in the baking process, so maybe you'd like to film me?" she said. She's such a show-off, and she's bossy too. She seems like the sort of person who would go around stealing other people's recipe books. (Unfortunately I can't accuse her without any proof just because she's totally annoying.)

Look at me!

She made the camera crew stay filming her for ages, talking about how she knew the best technique for creating the perfect rose flavored pink cupcake with pink icing.

Then the camera crew started to film Patsy Éclair, who was as cool as a cucumber.

"I'm going for a classic light and fluffy cupcake with a swirl of candy floss flavored icing," she said. "I can't bear a heavy sponge – only an amateur would make such a mistake."

Unbelievable!

She is so totally smug. I'm starting to think Violet is the only normal person in the competition.

SMUG ALERT

"I love your sparkly cupcake cases," Marie said to Violet on camera. "Where did you get them?"

sparkly

"My grandma gave them to me. She thinks they will help make my cupcakes look really mysterious," said Violet.

I could tell she wasn't really sure whether to look at the camera or at Marie.

Hmm, I thought. Why is Marie so interested in what Violet is doing? Is she a bit *too* interested? Could she have taken the recipe book? Next to Violet, she seems the nicest of the contestants, but it could be an elaborate trick.

After what seemed like no time at all, Spencer Spokes shouted, "Ten minutes, bakers. You have ten minutes left!"

Primula was on her knees shouting "RISE!" at the oven door. Marie Sloops was trying to open an enormous can of canned peaches, and Violet had accidentally showered herself in powdered sugar. She had all her cupcakes out of the oven, though, and if she could just get the icing on them, she'd be fine.

60

Patsy was the only one who didn't seem as if she was about to break under the pressure. She calmly removed her cupcakes from the oven and tipped them out. The cupcakes made a loud THUD as they landed on the worktop. Patsy started tapping them. Ha! What had she been saying about only amateurs making a heavy sponge?

THUD! (ha!)

If she's taken Grandma Maple's recipe book, she definitely hasn't read the chapter on light and fluffy sponges.

Oliver kept peering into one of his cupboards and checking his watch. What was he looking at in there? Grandma Maple's recipe book? I didn't have time to think about it for long because suddenly Oliver shouted, "Noooooooooooooo!"

He rushed to the oven, but he was too late. He pulled out a tray of smouldering black "volcano" cupcakes. The top of one of the cupcakes flew into the air and sprayed what looked like raspberry jam all over the top of the tent.

Oliver stood, helpless, as one by one the cakes exploded.

"I don't understand!" he wailed. "I checked the oven temperature three times. They weren't meant to explode until you bit into them!"

The banging and clattering noises in the kitchen were interrupted by the sound of Harriet Blythington ringing a small china bell. "That's it, bakers, time's up."

Dramatic music started to play again as one by one, the contestants took turns to bring their cakes to be tasted by the judges. Spencer Spokes and Harriet Blythington sampled Marie's cupcakes first. She'd made enough Fuzzy Peach cupcakes to feed seventy-five people.

"A good volume of cupcakes – interesting peachy decoration and the flavor," said Harriet, taking a mouthful, before immediately spitting it back out again. "Oh, my goodness! A hair! This cake has a hair in it!"

Hairy cakes

"But I had my hairnet on. Mom says to always wear a hairnet just in case. I don't know how this happened!" said Marie.

"Hair contamination might be commonplace in school dinners, but it has no place at Bake or Break," Spencer Spokes said sternly.

Things didn't seem to go well for any of the contestants.

Violet had done a wonderful job with her icing, but her cupcakes weren't cooked in the middle. Primula's cupcakes were beautifully decorated, but they were completely flat. The judges refused to taste Oliver's volcano cakes.

Harriet and Spencer looked as if they really didn't want to risk trying Patsy's cakes either. "This is the densest sponge I've ever had the misfortune to put in my mouth," said Harriet.

"And it tastes of … absolutely nothing," said Spencer Spokes.

"This really is the only semi-edible bake. It pains me to say it, but Patsy Éclair is the winner of the Cupcake Challenge," said Harriet Blythington. "You had better pull your socks up, finalists – we are expecting MUCH better things from you in the next challenge."

4:30 PM
OUTSIDE THE BAKE OR BREAK TENT

"Something strange is going on here. Not just what happened with the recipe book," said Violet.

BURNED

"Yes, bad luck on the raw cupcakes," said Poppy.

"LUCK! Luck has nothing to do with it, Poppy," said Violet, furious. "I know I set my oven to the right temperature. But when I checked again later, it had been turned down. And, doesn't it seem unusual to you that experienced bakers would all make simple mistakes like setting the oven too high or getting hair in the cupcakes?"

"Violet – are you saying that somebody has been messing with the ovens and putting hairs in people's cupcakes deliberately?" I asked.

"Yes, Mariella, I am. And that somebody is trying to ruin the other contestants' chances – not just mine," said Violet.

"This is serious. We could have a case of deliberate cupcake sabotage* on our hands," I said.

This competition is TOTALLY crazy! I was expecting to eat loads of really nice cupcakes and maybe give Violet a few motivational speeches. If all this has happened on Day One, who knows what could happen next?

*SABOTAGE: This is when you deliberately try to ruin something by messing with it or breaking it, or you turn an oven up to maximum temperature to burn someone's cakes. A person who sabotages something is called a "saboteur."

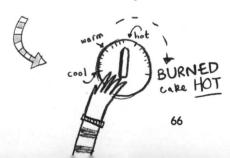

Tuesday
May 13th

BAKE OR BREAK FINALS,
DAY TWO:
THE PICNIC BASKET
CHALLENGE

THE PICNIC BASKET CHALLENGE
what will the judges pick?

KNOW YOUR SUSPECT:
How to Spot Suspicious Characters

Good detectives are able to spot suspicious characters instantly. Do you know what to look for? Practice using your powers of observation and it could help you to figure out who your key suspects are.

Suspicious behavior includes:

1. Looking flustered (as if they might have just been up to no good).

Sweating

Wild look in eyes

Dishevelled hair

2. Whistling innocently.
This can be a give-away that somebody is trying to cover up suspicious activity.

3. Having a shifty walk. You might see a suspect looking around every few seconds to check that they aren't being watched.

4. Running very quickly. Ask yourself – is this person exercising or could they be running from the scene of a crime?

Priceless Painting?

TOP TIP

Look out for anyone who appears to be concealing items under their clothing. They could have just stolen it from somewhere.

9:15 AM
22 SYCAMORE AVENUE, MY BEDROOM

After the incidents of what appeared to be
deliberate cupcake sabotage yesterday, we
called an emergency Mystery Girls team meeting
this morning.

We have narrowed down a list of our top
suspects, looked at the facts and tried to figure
out what their motive could be.

The saboteur probably thinks nobody knows
what they are up to. Well, they don't know much
about the Mystery Girls! We are onto them!

THE CUPCAKE CONUNDRUM: SUSPECTS
CUPCAKE SABOTEUR ACTIVITY SO FAR:

1. Violet Maple's recipe book has mysteriously vanished — was this because the saboteur knows she has a good chance of winning the competition and wants to stop her?

FLAT!

volcano cakes

2. Oven temperatures, ingredients and cake mixtures have been tampered with. These things happened so close together it seems unlikely that they are unrelated. We have deduced that the same person is responsible for both.

POSSIBLE MOTIVE:
All the Bake or Break contestants (apart from Violet) have a strong motive — they want to make sure they WIN Bake or Break.

TAMPERED

HOT

CHIEF SUSPECTS:

PATSY ÉCLAIR: She won the Cupcake Challenge so this should make her our only suspect — but her cakes showed signs of sabotage too. Did somebody tamper with her recipe, or did it go wrong because she was busy sabotaging other people's baking?

OLIVER PICKETT: Was he so busy destroying cakes he didn't notice his own cakes were burning? And what did he keep looking at in his cupboard? Grandma Maple's recipe book?

MARIE SLOOPS: Seems nice — is this an act? Told Violet she has to wait until she is older to get the Sloops Family recipe book. So has she taken Violet's? But there was quite a lot of hair in Marie's cake.

PRIMULA GORDON: I definitely saw her laugh about Violet being a Mystery Girl. And she told Violet she had probably lost her recipe book. Was this a cover-up? Actually, she did say she didn't need a recipe book because she already had loads of ideas. Was that a cover-up too? If she is the saboteur she got very distracted ruining all the other cakes — her cakes were horrible.

PROBABLY DIDN'T DO IT BUT NEED TO WATCH SUSPECTS:

HARRIET BLYTHINGTON AND SPENCER SPOKES:
They might be judges but you never know. Maybe they are trying to get more viewers by making the competition more difficult?

VERDICT: TRUST NOBODY

Poppy and I are going to pretend to do interviews for the school newspaper. We'll really be watching closely for unusual behavior and clues.

The Young Super Sleuth's Handbook says that if you're going to use a fake story to get information from people, you need to be convincing or your cover may be blown. I know loads of details about working at a newspaper because Dad is a journalist at the *Puddleford Gazette*. I went to work with him once and there were lots of people saying things like, "I need more coffee if I'm going to meet my deadline!" and "This feature has a typo!"

Violet's job is to keep her eyes and ears open for signs of cheating, and to get on with her awesome baking!

journalist cover

sheep

10:20 AM
BAKE OR BREAK TENT

Today the tent is decorated to tie in with the
Picnic Basket Challenge. There are loads of hay
bales and even a few sheep wandering around
the kitchens. It looks really nice and friendly, but
they aren't fooling me. Who knows what Bake or
Break will have in store for the contestants? And
who knows what the saboteur could be planning
to do next?

It's made me feel a bit better that Poppy is an
actual genius. She managed to find time last
night to make some totally amazing Team Violet
t-shirts. We are wearing them now. It sends
a message to the saboteur that Violet won't
be beaten.

I can't wait to see Violet's face when she sees us wearing them.

FRONT

KEEP CALM and concentrate on the cakes

Violet's head

THE mystery Girls For all your mystery solving needs

Back

We're going to start our fake interviews for the school newspaper now – with the contestants' parents. I'd like to think that as parents they wouldn't be encouraging their children to cheat. But there's a chance they might know something – and maybe even be in on the cheating. I'm starting to think anything is possible. Report back soon.

Read our totally cool interviews

INTERVIEWS: CONTESTANTS' PARENTS

MRS. GORDON (PRIMULA'S MOM): Seemed very eager to be featured in the school paper. (Obviously a show-off, just like Primula.) Said, "Primmy's made plans for a huge celebration party when she wins!" When she wins? Is Primula so sure she is going to win because she is going to make sure nobody else has a chance?

MRS. SLOOPS (MOTHER OF MARIE): Didn't seem to have anything to hide. Said Marie would be wearing two hairnets today, just to be completely sure there are no hair-related incidents. (Talked about school dinners for ages.)

MR. AND MRS. PICKETT (OLIVER'S PARENTS):

Said Oliver's been experimenting with recipes for weeks. He keeps his experiments top secret in case anybody tries to copy them. Interesting. He could be plotting anything in his laboratory, like a cunning plan of SABOTAGE!

MRS. ÉCLAIR (PATSY'S MOM):

Said Patsy's "raw baking talent" is easy to see. (Really?) Also said Patsy was extremely mature for her age, unlike the other contestants. (She stared hard at our Team Violet t-shirts when she said that. RUDE!)

We've gathered lots of pieces of incriminating evidence, but nothing that makes one person look more guilty than the next. These contestants are just WEIRD!

The Picnic Basket

11:00 AM
PICNIC BASKET CHALLENGE IS ABOUT
TO START!

Poppy and I have got our Young Super Sleuth
binoculars ready – we aren't going to miss a
thing. So we don't forget anything that could
be important later, I'm going to write down
everything as it happens:

me, solving
the mystery!

PICNIC BASKET CHALLENGE

10:30 AM: Spencer Spokes pulls a slip of paper out of the giant picnic basket. The contestants must all bake a lemon meringue pie.

10:39 AM: After a LONG lecture from Harriet on the correct techniques for meringue whipping, the contestants begin to bake.

10:52 AM: Oliver seems stressed. He's looking in that cupboard again. Poppy tries to adjust magnification on our

X-RAY Glasses

binoculars, but it's no good. (Must ask for Young Super Sleuth X-ray glasses as birthday present.)

11:02 AM: Marie gets over-excited with her electric whisk and sprays meringue on Violet's face. Is this deliberate? Violet doesn't even look up. Our Mystery Girl preparations were worth it!

whisko

11:17 AM: Patsy's mom turns around and asks Violet's mom to tell Poppy and me to  stop whispering and waving binoculars around. Violet's mom says we are just enjoying the show and makes a face at Mrs. Éclair when she turns away.

11:23 AM: Oliver has made a screen around his pie from tea towels. He says his meringue topping must remain unseen until he reveals the finished pie. Is he doing something else behind those tea towels? Like preparing disgusting flavors to put in other people's cakes?

11:25 AM: Violet does a fantastic job of explaining to Harriet that she is going for "flavor over fanciness" (that's another one of Grandma Maple's tips). Harriet says Violet's pie has all the qualities of a winning pie and it's the best she's seen so far.

the best

11:30 AM: *No evidence of deliberate sabotage to report yet. Oven temperatures remain stable.*

11:35 AM: Primula says very loudly, "MY GOODNESS! My meringue is so massive I don't think it will fit in the oven!" She babbles on to the cameras about her whipping technique. She'll do anything to get on TV.

11:52 AM: Patsy takes some very small lemon meringue pies out of the oven. She tells the cameras, "Pies are so unsophisticated. These are mini lemon meringue tartlets." She is so smug. I bet she actually thinks she is the Icing on the Cake – Poppy says she is an Ice Queen, not the icing queen. (Ha.)

11:55 AM: Time is up and the pies are displayed for the judges to taste.

ICE
QUEEN

THE PIES!

MARIE: Looks big enough to feed a whole school cafeteria full of people.

51.5 cm

VIOLET: Edible glitter makes the pie look really exciting and a bit mysterious!

glitter

PATSY: Mini tartlets (or whatever she calls them). Doesn't look like enough to me.

huger!

PRIMULA: Pie is so big she can't lift it onto its cake stand without help.

OLIVER: He's recreated the face of Harriet Blythington in the meringue topping. WOW!

11:57 AM: Spencer Spokes says he can't possibly judge the cakes after working so hard all morning, and calls a lunch break. **MYSTERY GIRLS DEDUCTION:** He's jealous he didn't get his face made from meringue.

12:50 PM
BAKE OR BREAK TENT

A lunch break couldn't have come at a better time — we've managed to catch up with Violet. She says she hasn't experienced anything suspicious, but we need to wait until the judges have tasted the pies to check that nothing has actually happened.

I told Violet that I have deduced the cupcake saboteur is lying low so they don't arouse suspicion. Violet did point out that this could mean there isn't a cupcake saboteur at all and maybe her recipe book did just go missing and the cupcakes were a disaster yesterday because the bakers were nervous.

I know I should hope that Violet is right. It would be better for her if nobody was cheating and I really do want her to win the competition because it's her dream. But it's been a while since we had a really big mystery and it would be wonderful if we could solve this. (If it is, in fact, a mystery.)

Hang on. **HUGE** crash has just come from the tent! Must investigate.

winners
trophy

6:00 PM
MYSTERY GIRLS HQ

TOTAL BAKING SABOTAGE ALERT!

I can confirm we are now absolutely certain there is a baking saboteur at work. This is my first chance to report what had happened:

CASE REPORT:
SCENE OF THE SMUSH

12:53 PM: After hearing a loud crash from the kitchen area the Mystery Girls are first on the scene. We uncover a shocking act of pie sabotage. Violet screams.

ARRRGH!

12:54 PM: Her lemon meringue pie is lying next to Marie's in a smushed-up-pie mess on the floor. The side of the tent has blown open and is flapping in the wind.

smushed!

12:55 PM: The other contestants rush into the kitchen area followed by Harriet Blythington and Spencer Spokes. Marie shouts, "MY PIE! WHO DID THAT TO MY PIE?"

12:57 PM: Harriet says how unfortunate it is that Violet and Marie's pies appear to have been blown over in a "freak gust of wind." She says nobody would have pushed the pies over deliberately because that type of thing doesn't happen at Bake or Break.

wind?

1:05 PM: Judges say that the cakes must still be judged because Rule 502 states: "Bake or Break cannot be held responsible for any accidental dropping, squashing, or falling over of cakes, pies, and pastries baked by contestants."

1:10 PM: Harriet and Spencer say polite things about the flavor of Marie and Violet's cakes even though they look like heaps of mushed-up yellow goo.

1:15 PM: Oliver says his pie is a tribute to the meringue genius of Harriet Blythington. Patsy is criticized for having no lemon in her lemon meringue tartlets. She looks disgusted.

1:20 PM: Spencer Spokes is about to take a spoonful of Primula's enormous pie when a voice comes from inside it: "Help me!"

1:21 PM: Harriet Blythington prods the cake and the top flaps open. Primula's little sister, Charlotte, sticks her head out. She is sobbing and covered in lemon goo. The audience gasps. (We totally weren't expecting that.)

Argggh!

goo!

totally shocking

1:25 PM: Primula tries to explain to the judges that her sister was supposed to leap out of the pie in a show-stopping baking moment. Primula admits she sneaked in at lunchtime to conceal her sister, before the "freak gust of wind" blew everyone's pies over. (Totally probably not true!)

1:30 PM: The judges disqualify Primula from this round for adding extra ingredients after the time limit was up. Primula stamps her foot and shouts, "But that's not fair!" (Neither is cheating. Ha! Serves her right!)

1:32 PM: The judges announce that Oliver is the winner of the Picnic Basket Challenge. Patsy shouts, "Oh WHATEVER, as if I care!" and storms off stage. (Angrily!)

Angry!

VERDICT: THERE WAS NO FREAK GUST OF WIND. THE BAKING SABOTEUR IS STILL AT WORK. (AND IT LOOKS HIGHLY LIKELY IT IS PRIMULA GORDON.)

Only serious mysteries need emergency Mystery
Girl team meetings and we've just had our
second one in two days. This is crazy. We need
to stop Primula from doing anything else to
ruin Violet's chances. (I knew I didn't like her the
moment I saw her.)

Violet looked completely miserable.
"I don't like this, girls," she said.
"If it is Primula trying to ruin
everyone's chances, she
is really mean. That
was the best lemon
meringue pie I'd ever
made and it ended
up as mush."

miserable

"It was obvious that the cakes had been pushed over, even before we knew Primula had sneaked back inside at lunchtime," said Poppy.

"Obvious to us," I said. "Not everyone is a totally ace Young Super Sleuth, though. Our main suspect did another good job of making it look like an accident."

"I may as well give up!" Violet said. "You heard what Harriet said – 'Cheating doesn't happen at Bake or Break'."

"I'm sure we can persuade her, Violet, " I said. "And cheer up, just think of the look on Primula's face when she was disqualified. Her plan totally backfired!"

If Harriet knew about the missing recipe book and the cake sabotage in the first challenge, I'm sure she'd reconsider what had really happened to the lemon meringue pies. Wouldn't she?

92

-camera

7:35 PM
MYSTERY GIRLS HQ, THE MYSTERY DESK

We've just analyzed the photos we took before
Violet had to scrape up her pie from the floor,
and I can confirm we now have strong evidence
that this was no accident. It's not quite concrete
evidence* yet because we haven't actually got a
photo of Primula red-handed. I wish I'd noticed
all the clues back at the tent, but everything
happened so quickly.

*CONCRETE EVIDENCE: Some very solid
evidence that proves without any doubt
that somebody did something.
→ evidence

SCENE OF THE SMUSH: PHOTOGRAPHIC ANALYSIS

Pies untouched by the "freak gust of wind." (Not what usually happens during a freak gust of wind.)

smush!

VIOLET'S PIE: Meringue splatter is toward the side of tent: if the cake was blown over it would have splatted the other way.

MARIE'S PIE: Fell off other side of the table to Violet's. Surely it should have fallen the same way if it was blown off?

tornado

WEATHER CONDITIONS TODAY: Calm and still — no sudden tornadoes forecast as far as we know.

This evidence suggests Primula sneaked into the kitchens – not just to hide her sister in her pie, but also to destroy Violet and Marie's. I can't believe this happened right under our noses.

"Hang on," Poppy said. "If Primula is the baking saboteur, why did she only ruin Violet and Marie's cakes? Oliver and Patsy's cakes were competition, too."

"Maybe she only meant to destroy Violet's pie and Marie's got pushed off by accident?" I said. "Everyone heard Harriet say how good Violet's pie was – that makes her a huge threat to Primula."

"Or maybe Primula went crazy with pie jealousy, threw the plates on the floor and then had to run off before she finished the job because she made so much noise smashing plates," said Poppy.

Violet leaped up. "I can't believe she said I'd just lost my recipe book when she really stole it. She could be reading my Mystery Maple Marvel recipe right now. If I don't get that recipe back before the Show-Stopper Challenge I've got no chance! WE HAVE TO STOP HER!"

Wow. Go, Violet! This is what being a Mystery Girl is all about – searching for the truth and stopping terrible acts of cake sabotage.

THE MYSTERY GIRLS
? DETERMINED ?
FEARLESS!
AMAZING ?

we are totally ACE!

we can SOLVE ANY mystery

my totally
serious
face

8:00 PM
MYSTERY GIRLS HQ, INTRUDER ALERT

We were all looking really serious because we were solving a VERY serious mystery, when a squeaky voice broke the silence ...

"Mariiiieellllaaaa! Look at me! Look at this!"

Arthur was wobbling into the yard wearing one of his stupid costumes – a giant padded cupcake with pink icing on. He clearly couldn't see where he was going very well because he almost ran into a tree. He is so embarrassing.

"Mom said you'd love it!" he cried. "We found it in the attic. She said it used to be yours!"

what!?

Unfortunately, I did recognize the costume. But I'm a totally cool detective now so I don't want anyone knowing I used to dress up as a giant cupcake.

"I don't know what you are talking about!" I yelled. "I've never seen that stupid cake before."

"Actually, Mariella, I remember it," said Poppy. "You wore it to my fifth birthday party."

"I remember that too!" said Violet, smiling for the first time since her pie was sabotaged.

Sometimes it's difficult to be a brilliant Young Super Sleuth when your friends are detectives too. Poppy and Violet have trained their brains to remember important clues. This means that they can remember every embarrassing thing you ever did before you were a serious detective.

Wednesday May 14th

BAKE OR BREAK FINALS,
DAY THREE:
Children's Party Challenge

Mission: Convince Harriet and Spencer that Primula is a MASSIVE cheat.

9:25 AM
BAKE OR BREAK TENT,
VIP AUDIENCE AREA

Poppy, Violet, and I arrived really early today to talk to Harriet Blythington and Spencer Spokes. I wish Violet would hurry up. She's gone backstage to find them. I can hardly bear to look at the team of Bake or Break mascots in black leotards and tutus practicing throwing empty paper plates. Soon those plates will be filled with cream and if the contestants make even one mistake – SPLAT – it'll be all over their faces.

party hats

tutu

10:02 AM
BAKE OR BREAK TENT, LYING LOW

Things aren't going according to plan. First Violet
sent us this note from backstage:

Spencer Spokes is having his hair
styled — hairdressing team won't let
me near him. Harriet is busy preparing
her special announcement. Worried
she'll send someone home for being
horrible (Me). Will keep trying to
speak to judges. Got to go, got to
prepare Mystery Macaroon ingredients.
Worried.

mystery macaroons

Violet xx

hair spray

Then, while Poppy and I were trying to figure out how on earth we were going to speak to the judges, we were interrupted by a familiar voice coming from the big screen in the kitchens.

"Yay! I'm so glad to be here with the Mystery Girls. Is this going to be on TV?"

ARTHUR! I tried to act cool, like I didn't know who he was, in case anyone was watching.

"WHAT is he doing here?" I said to Poppy.

Arthur
↓
no!

"Oh, sorry, Mariella," said Violet's mom. "Your mom texted me to say she was dropping him off. Your dad got some free last-minute tickets from the *Puddleford Gazette!*"

NO! This is terrible. If the judges see him
messing around, they are never going to take
us seriously.

"My favorite contestant is Violet. She's great! She's
like my best friend!" said Arthur, beaming and
waving his Bake or Break Annual. "I'm a Mystery
Girl too!"

I cannot believe Mom and Dad sent him here.
Arthur overheard me telling them about how
Primula is our main suspect and started asking
loads of annoying questions. Now he'll be bugging
me all day and probably shouting things like,
"PRIMULA DID IT!"

Arggggghhhhhh!

Hang on – we've just heard Harriet's special
announcement. Workspace inspections! She'll be
awarding extra points for bakers who show an
organized kitchen. Well, that's easy. Violet can
handle this, no problem.

Violet's organized kitchen →

Oh no, wait ...

There was a second announcement! A Change of Challenge. The final challenge isn't going to be the Show Stopper after all – it's going to be a Drum Challenge. This is when contestants get a random ingredient out of a revolving drum and have to bake a cake using it. One year, a boy ended up "breaking" when he couldn't think of a cake to bake using spaghetti. He lay on the floor and wiggled about, insisting he was actually a piece of spaghetti. It was awful to watch.

Violet is probably having a Maple Meltdown right now.

THE DRUM CHALLENGE

open

DISASTER! The worst thing EVER has happened to the Mystery Girls. I have been framed – framed for trying to sabotage Bake or Break!

We were waiting for the workspace inspections to start and everything seemed fine. No obvious sabotage activity or anything, until Violet opened her cupboard. She shot Poppy and me a look that said, "I need Mystery Girl help NOW!"

HELP!

The Look

When we got to Violet she shoved a bag in my hand and whispered, "Here, take this. I think Primula is trying to frame me!"

My detective instincts kicked in. I shoved the bag under my Team Violet t-shirt and grabbed Poppy's arm. We needed to get the bag away from the judges – NOW!

As we headed for the exit, Primula tried to intercept us. She wants the bag! I thought.

"I've heard all about your school newspaper. I was wondering if you'd like to write a feature about me?" said Primula.

"Got to run, deadline to meet!" I said. She wasn't going to fool me that easily.

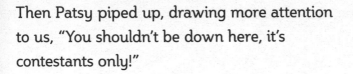

Then Patsy piped up, drawing more attention to us, "You shouldn't be down here, it's contestants only!"

We were almost at the exit when one of the Bake or Break crew stepped in front of us and told us to take our seats. Filming was about to begin. I wish now I'd just kept running but I couldn't risk drawing any more attention to me and Poppy – and the bag.

The workspace inspections seemed to last forever. Harriet was going on and on about specks of dust on tea towels and crumbs on the floor. Eventually the Children's Party Challenge started but all I could think was, what could be in the bag to make Violet look guilty?

Suddenly, the tent started to fill with thick black smoke.

A voice sounded over the speakers:

"BURNED CAKE ALERT.
BURNED CAKE ALERT
EVACUATE THE TENT!"

"Mariella, run!" Poppy said, leaping out of her seat.

This was it, my opportunity to get the bag out (of the tent). As I sprinted into the entrance hall I turned to see if Poppy was behind me – and ran straight into Patsy's mom. It was like she appeared from nowhere.

I fell and the bag slipped out from under my t-shirt ...

It skidded across the floor and a little stuffed bear with a chef's hat rolled out. That doesn't look very incriminating, I thought.

Then Oliver shouted, "IT WAS YOU! You stole my lucky mascot, Mr. Bunsworth, from MY cupboard!"

So that's what he kept looking at in there. Then I realized I was in what the Young Super Sleuth's Handbook would call a very Sticky Situation.

A crowd started to gather and before I could stop her, Mrs. Éclair passed the judges the bag of planted evidence and said, "Harriet, Spencer, you need to take a look at this."

THIS IS WHAT WAS IN THE BAG ...

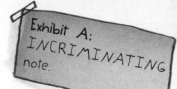

Exhibit A: INCRIMINATING note.

WAYS TO SABOTAGE COMPETITION

1. TAMPER WITH OVENS SO THEY ARE SO HOT THEY BURN THE CAKES.

2. PUT HAIRS IN PEOPLE'S CAKES — HA!

3. DESTROY AS MANY LEMON MERINGUE PIES AS POSSIBLE.

HAIR!

chilis

Exhibit B: Bag of hairs

Exhibit C: Bag of extra spicy chilis

Exhibit D: Mr. Bunsworth (bear mascot of Oliver's)

BEAR

I tried to explain about Primula, but nobody would listen. One of the crew recognized me from the auditions and said I must have wanted to sabotage the competition because I didn't get into the finals. Spencer Spokes said he had never seen such outrageous cheating. Then Harriet banned me (and Poppy, because it looked bad that she was with me) from ever returning to Bake or Break.

I am too distraught to write anything else. (Apart from PRIMULA GORDON IS A MASSIVE CHEATER!!!)

ADVANCED DETECTIVE WORK: FALSE ACCUSATIONS

Suspects won't be very happy that you are about to uncover what they have done, and in rare circumstances the suspect might try to make you look as if you don't know what you are doing. That way nobody will believe a thing you say and the suspect will get away with what they have done. Don't worry! There are things you can do to persuade people that you are telling the truth.

Why not try . . .?

1. Finding a piece of very strong, or **concrete evidence** to prove your suspect did it.

2. Catch your suspect **red-handed**, and take a photo.

3. Make a **poster** listing all the brilliant mysteries you have solved in the past, show this to anyone who doesn't believe what you are saying to show you are a trustworthy person.

DISCOVER FAMOUS DETECTIVES:

The career of renowned detective, Fifi the Sneaker, was almost shattered when a false accusation was made against her.

Fifi had uncovered a plot by a group of highly organized criminals to stage the world's biggest panty heist. Unfortunately, the gang had figured out Fifi was on to them. After raiding the Big Bloomers panty factory the gang left one of Fifi's signature red berets in place of the panties they had just stolen.

Fifi arrived on the scene too late to stop the theft but just in time to be accused of the crime by the police.

Thinking quickly, Fifi mananged to track a trail of panties from the factory right back to the gang's headquarters. The gang was arrested after being caught red-handed unloading their stolen goods. (They intended to sell the panties for huge sums of money by pretending they were the undergarments of famous people.)

TOP TIP

If everything else fails, lie low for a while, change your name and start a new detective agency ...

me ↓
Poppy

← us being kicked out.

3:30 PM
MYSTERY GIRLS HQ, NOT SURE WHAT TO DO

Even though Violet didn't get kicked out with me and Poppy, this could be the end of her chances in the competition. Everyone knows she is friends with us, and if she doesn't get disqualified for that, there's still Primula to worry about.

But worse, much worse (and I can tell Poppy is thinking the same thing although neither of us want to admit it), this could be the end of the Mystery Girls. Who is going to trust a group of mystery-solvers who have been banned from a competition for cheating? NOBODY!

Poppy is trying to find a page in the Young Super Sleuths' Handbook that tells us what to do in this sort of situation. She's looking in the advanced section. We need a plan, and quickly.

WARNING!

AVOID AT ALL COSTS:
Mariella Mystery and Poppy Holmes

DO NOT APPROACH. They are wanted in connection with serious incidents of attempted cake sabotage. They are known to be dangerous (if you are baking).

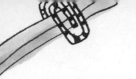

5:03 PM
MYSTERY GIRLS HQ (WITH ARTHUR, ARRRGGH!)

Some new evidence has come to light – I still can't quite believe who helped us get it.

Poppy and I had been trying to think of a plan in Mystery Girls HQ for ages when Violet ran into the yard with Arthur behind her. She'd just finished the Children's Party Challenge.

"Are you all right?" Violet shouted up to us. "I'm so sorry for giving you the bag!"

"Don't be silly, Violet," I said. "At least Primula didn't manage to frame you."

"What happened? Did you get to bake the Mystery Macaroons? Did Primula try anything else?" Poppy said.

"That's just it – it isn't Primula who tried to frame me. Primula isn't the saboteur!" said Violet.

What? I was sure Violet must have got it wrong.

"Yeah, I've got new information!" said Arthur.

"Stop messing around, Arthur, this is serious stuff," I said. "Violet, tell us everything."

"He's not messing around! He really did get new information. It's important," said Violet.

Today was turning out to be totally weird. Now Arthur was supposed to have done something useful. There would need to be strong evidence to make me believe Primula didn't do it after the clues we've found.

CASE REPORT: ARTHUR'S NEW INFORMATION

1:05 PM: Arthur is bored. Since Poppy and I are banned from ever returning to Bake or Break, he has nobody to talk to.

1:10 PM: Spotting a girl his own age, Arthur goes to talk to her. Arthur realizes the girl is Charlotte, Primula's sister, but thinks she seems nice anyway.

Arthur

Charlotte

1:15 PM: Arthur and Charlotte sit and read Arthur's Bake or Break Annual. Arthur says he is on Team Violet and hopes she wins. Charlotte says she hopes Violet wins too, because her sister Primula is horrible.

1:20 PM: Charlotte tells Arthur how Primula made her get inside the giant lemon meringue pie even though she got covered in goo.

goo

1:22 PM: Arthur asks if Primula pushed over the other pies. (Good work, Arthur!) Charlotte says all Primula cared about was stuffing Charlotte inside her meringue.

1:25 PM: Charlotte says she was sitting inside the pie when she heard footsteps, then lots of crashing and splatting. She tried to open the pie, but the meringue topping had got stuck to the base. She shouted, "Help! Please help me!" Then the footsteps started running away.

1:26 PM: Charlotte was so upset by the time Harriet Blythington managed to open the meringue that she couldn't say anything about what had happened. Primula blames Charlotte for getting her disqualified and they aren't speaking, so Charlotte doesn't see why she should tell her sister anything.

dinner

6:15 PM
THE KITCHEN TABLE, 22 SYCAMORE AVENUE
(MY HOUSE)

Mom made me come inside for dinner.
(Apparently I look pale after this afternoon's
dramatic incident and so need to eat some
vegetables.)

Arthur's new evidence has definitely made it
seem as if Primula isn't the saboteur. So who is it?

I managed to get these facts about the Birthday
Cake Challenge from Violet. They could reveal an
important clue.

CHILDREN'S PARTY CHALLENGE — THE FACTS

The atmosphere was tense after Poppy and
I were framed. When Marie tried to start a
conversation with Violet, Primula said, "Don't
talk to Violet. Her friends are CHEATERS!"

Before the contestants were allowed to carry
on with the challenge, Harriet gave them
a lecture about cheating and how it was
completely unacceptable and would not be
tolerated on Bake or Break.

Nobody was sure where the smoke had
come from because no cakes had been
burned or anything. Spencer Spokes
said the smoke machine must have
been acting up.

When the challenge started again,
Violet said that Patsy's Eiffel
Tower cake looked amazing.
Earlier it had seemed
like she had loads to
do, but now it really
did look like the
Eiffel Tower.

Eiffel
Tower →
cake

sponge

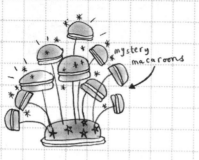

mystery
macaroons

Violet managed to arrange her Mystery Macaroons to look like a mysterious formation of flying UFOs.
She thought it was impressive until she put it next to Patsy's cake.

The Bake or Break mascots decided they didn't like Primula's Pink Palace of Iced Buns, so they chucked a cream pie at her. She went ballistic, screaming and flinging iced buns into the audience.

buns

Primula

SMUG

ALERT

Patsy won the challenge. The judges said her cake showed real style and sophistication. Patsy just said, "Of course it has style and sophistication, I baked it." SMUG ALERT!

I've been so busy focusing on Primula, maybe I've been missing what Patsy has been up to. There's something suspicious about the way she managed to pull her Eiffel Tower cake together at the last minute. Did she have help?

Oliver could easily have put the bag of fake evidence containing Mr. Bunsworth in Violet's cupboard,

and he is VERY secretive. But is he too much of a wimp to have carried out the totally shocking acts of sabotage we've seen so far?

We don't think Marie is the culprit. Her pie was definitely pushed and you wouldn't sabotage your own pie if you were trying to win.

Anyway, whoever it is, nobody is going to believe the Mystery Girls unless we can catch them red-handed. That means Poppy and I have to find a way to get back into Bake or Break.

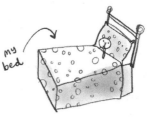

my bed

8:08 PM
MY BEDROOM (22 SYCAMORE AVENUE)

Tomorrow is the last day of the competition. It's our last chance to solve the Cupcake Conundrum.

Violet is worried about what's going to happen during the Drum Challenge. Only a really experienced baker will be able to invent a recipe on the spot. I know Violet can do that but she isn't so sure. It would be great if Violet could win just one of the challenges. Her lemon meringue pie came so close – it's not her fault it got smushed by the saboteur.

eggs

Violet isn't giving up, that's the main thing. She's been writing down the mysterious recipes she's baked in the competition so far. She's going to stick them in her grandma's recipe book (if we ever get it back). She's hoping her final recipe will be as delicious as the Mystery

recipes

Maple Marvel was going to be. It all depends on what she pulls out of the (dreaded) drum.

It's going to be difficult, but this is what we need to do to solve the Cupcake Conundrum tomorrow:

1: Infiltrate* the Bake or Break tent by wearing a cunning disguise. Violet can't win the competition and solve the mystery on her own.

cunning disguise

2: Get **conclusive proof** to show Harriet and Spencer by catching the cake saboteur red-handed. They are sure to attempt one final act of sabotage tomorrow to make sure they win. (And we can't wait until they win to find out who the saboteur is, because by then it will be too late to stop them!)

3: Clear the good name of the Mystery Girls.

*INFILTRATE: Get inside a place where you aren't supposed to be (Bake or Break) without anyone realizing you are there.

we are innocent!

Thursday May 15th

BAKE OR BREAK FINALS,
DAY FOUR:
The DRUM Challenge

Mission: STOP this madness!

Too busy being in love with himself to notice a CHEAT is at work

I am SO beautiful

12:03 AM
MY BEDROOM, 22 SYCAMORE AVENUE
(ACTUALLY IN BED)

I need to get to sleep but my head is spinning.
I've been doing some more Bake or Break
research and have just found this. (I hope Arthur
won't notice I've ripped the page out of his book.)

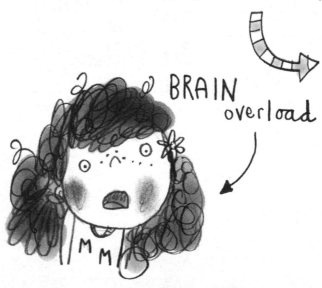

BRAIN overload

BAKE OR BREAK –
THE YEAR OF THE SCANDAL

We've told you about the spectacular "breaks" Bake or Break has seen over the years, as competitors melt under the pressures of some of the most demanding baking challenges ever seen on television. But that isn't the worst of it.

One year, junior contestant, Valerie Boggins, went to extraordinary lengths to ensure she would be Champion Baker. Accomplished bakers found their ovens mysteriously turned up to maximum temperature, salt mistaken for sugar and buns that toppled off cake stands (apparently by themselves).

Mysteriously burned cake incident

Rumors began to circulate that something suspicious was going on – that somebody was sabotaging the bakers' work.

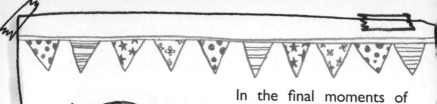

Valerie Boggins caught red-handed!

In the final moments of the competition, Valerie was caught red-handed by Harriet Blythington trying to switch her burned cake with a perfect cake she'd had made by a French patisserie. Valerie was disqualified from the competition and banned from ever returning to Bake or Break.

The audience was very concerned that a cheater came so close to winning, and at one point the series was nearly cancelled. If it hadn't been for the tireless work of Harriet Blythington persuading TV bosses to give the show a second chance, it could have been the end for Bake or Break.

The winner! Success overshadowed by scandal.

Wow! So this isn't the first time there has been sabotage at Bake or Break! I thought it was strange that Harriet refused to believe there was cheating going on. It caused such a scandal last time, she obviously doesn't want to admit it is happening again. The Young Super Sleuths' Handbook says it's important to face up to a problem – if you don't, then things can get out of hand. It looks like they already are at Bake or Break.

Valerie Boggins looks sort of familiar. Maybe it's just the crazed look in her eyes. I've seen that look from most of the contestants this year. This competition is CRAZY!

CRAZED contestant

DISGUISES AND COSTUMES

Detective work can be very serious at times, so why not have some fun designing your own disguises and costumes? Get a detective wardrobe prepared – you never know when you might need a disguise. Here are a few ideas to get you started:

A pantomime horse (perfect for team mystery solving)

Keep a **selection of wigs** in your Mystery Kit for emergencies:

sleek

beehive

Elvis

swoopy hair

bob

Realistic **tree outfit**

Fake beard and quirky hat!

TOP TIP

Remember, in most cases you'll need a disguise because you are going undercover. This means you won't want to draw too much attention to yourself – avoid bright colors and shiny fabrics.

Why not try being a superhero?

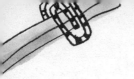

8:15 AM
MYSTERY GIRLS HQ

Violet says the Bake or Break people have been warned we might try and sneak in, so we are going to pretend to be official mascots sent from Head Office. Poppy remembered the cake costume Arthur was wearing the other day (I'd tried to forget about it) and had the genius idea of using it as a disguise. It turns out Arthur has quite a collection of cake-themed outfits in his costume box. We are going undercover – as giant cakes. I am Agent Cupcake and Poppy is Agent Donut.

cupcake

donut

Poppy has made very convincing fake Bake or Break Official Mascot badges for us both. We'll just wave them at the security guards and they'll be sure to let us in.

The cake outfit is actually very useful. It provides a brilliant top secret location to write in this journal, because nobody can see what I am up to! And there's loads of room inside to store things – I've got the Mystery Kit in here and some extra things we might need:

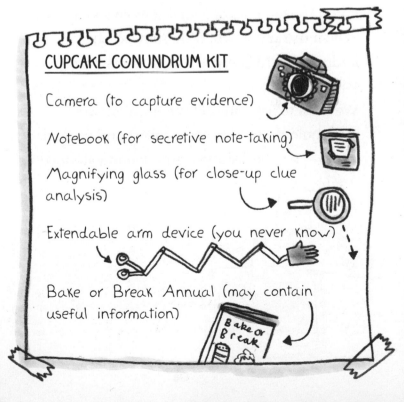

CUPCAKE CONUNDRUM KIT

Camera (to capture evidence)

Notebook (for secretive note-taking)

Magnifying glass (for close-up clue analysis)

Extendable arm device (you never know)

Bake or Break Annual (may contain useful information)

9:52 AM
BAKE OR BREAK TENT, BACKSTAGE AREA

Even though pretending to be mascots to sneak into the competition was risky, it was TOTALLY exciting. The Bake or Break staff checking tickets just let us right in when we showed our fake badges. The Mystery Girls – masters of disguise!

We tried to act natural (as natural as we could dressed as huge cakes) and walked backstage – and nobody stopped us!

our ID badges

OFFICIAL MASCOT ACCESS ALL AREAS

OFFICIAL MASCOT ACCESS ALL AREAS

Today the tent is set up to look like a fun fair for the Drum Challenge. There is a big spiral slide in the corner and a huge sign with flashing lights that says "Bake or Break – THE DRUM CHALLENGE." It's amazing how well our costumes blend in.

"Agent Cupcake, Oliver at one o'clock, I repeat, Oliver at one o'clock," said Poppy. Oliver was sitting talking to his mom and dad.

We shuffled a bit closer so we could hear what Oliver was saying. Poppy started pretending to make the letters of Bake or Break using her arms. This felt a bit silly, but it was all part of our cover.

"Don't worry, son. If it gets too stressful, you can give Mr. Bunsworth a cuddle and he'll bring you extra good luck," Oliver's mom was saying.

Oliver pulled out Mr. Bunsworth and gave him a loving squeeze.

"I love you, Mr. Bunsworth," I heard him whisper.

bit soppy

"Agent Donut," I said as we walked away. "Would a highly skilled and ruthless cake saboteur cuddle their lucky mascot in public?"

"I don't think so," said Poppy. "Come to think of it, would they even have a bear mascot called Mr. Bunsworth?"

"I think it's unlikely, Agent Donut. Let's see what else we can uncover."

10:10 AM
BAKE OR BREAK TENT, AVOIDING PRIMULA

I don't know why we didn't think of wearing a disguise sooner. It's a great way to eavesdrop on conversations. We overheard Marie's mom running through a list with her of unusual ingredients that you can add to a cake and still make it taste nice.

We also spied Primula. She didn't seem to be doing anything suspicious. When a TV camera came near her, she started showing off. She's obviously gotten over her Pink Palace of Iced Buns tantrum.

"I'm just sooooo excited about the final challenge.
I love drum raffles and I love winning things! Oh,
and I love cakes!" she said, grabbing hold of
my arm.

For a moment I thought Primula had figured
it out, that she knew it was me inside the cake
costume. Then I realized she was laughing her
head off. Phew! She made Poppy and me stay
waving at the camera for ages while she messed
around pretending to take bites out of our
costumes. Eurrrgh. Get lost! We've got important
mystery-solving to do.

10:20 AM
BAKE OR BREAK TENT, TRACKING THE ÉCLAIRS

I was starting to get really worried that we were running out of time. If we didn't find out who the saboteur was soon, they were going to get away with it. But something very interesting has just happened.

"Patsy is talking to her mom. I repeat, Patsy is talking to her mom," said Poppy.

Patsy's mom kept glancing around, like she was making sure that nobody could hear what she was saying. Patsy looked as if she was in a bad mood. (No change there then.)

BAD MOOD!

"You've come this far. DON'T let all our hard work go to waste. You could win this competition," Mrs. Éclair was whispering (quite loudly, I thought).

totally annoyed

"Oh, whatever, Valerie. If you hadn't messed up, this would be a done deal by now," said Patsy, giving her mom one of her Ice Queen glares.

Messed up? Messed up what? I thought.

"I've told you before, darling," said Patsy's mom. "Please stop calling me by my first name. It's Mother, OK?"

TOTALLY ANNOYED!

Valerie. Why does that name sound familiar? Then Patsy made a face at her mom and stormed off.

10:30 AM
BAKE OR BREAK TENT,
INGREDIENTS' STORAGE AREA

I pulled Poppy into a storage area — we had to
figure out what Patsy and her mom were talking
about.

"Poppy! Patsy is annoyed that her mom messed
something up! What do you think it could be?"
I asked.

"I don't know, Mariella," Poppy said, looking
confused.

I sat down on some bags of flour.
I needed to think. What did
Patsy's mom mean? Messed up?

OUCH!

inside the cupcake

Arthur's Bake or Break Annual
toppled over inside my
costume, prodding into my side.

"Did you hear Patsy call her
mom by her first name? Valerie!"
Poppy said. "She was so rude."

Valerie … the Bake or Break Annual … Of course!
I knew that face was familiar.

I showed Poppy the photo of Valerie Boggins,
the known cake saboteur from the Bake or Break
Annual. Surely it was too much of a coincidence
that there were two people called Valerie linked
to the competition who both seemed to be
involved with cheating?

Valerie
Boggins

Valerie Éclair

144

"Valerie Boggins and Valerie Éclair are the same person, Poppy. I think the Valerie who was disqualified all those years ago has come back with her daughter to try and win!" I said.

"To win by cheating again!" said Poppy.

"Exactly," I said. "But what has Valerie messed up? That could be important."

"Patsy has won two out of the three rounds, so her mom hasn't messed up too much," said Poppy. "Apart from the lemon meringue pie round."

"That must be it – Patsy is annoyed with her mom for not destroying all the lemon meringue pies," I said, staring at Poppy. (It felt a bit weird, as all I could see was a giant donut.)

giant donut

"Whoa," said Poppy. "If she'd won that round as well, she would have been almost impossible to beat in the final challenge."

Have we really just solved the Cupcake Conundrum? This is the bit where we usually celebrate because everyone believes us and is really grateful to us for solving the mystery. But this case is different. The judges won't believe Patsy and Valerie are up to no good just because we say so.

We need to find some concrete evidence, and fast.

10:42 PM
BAKE OR BREAK TENT, KITCHEN AREA

We made our way past the TV crew, who were busy with clipboards and moving cameras around. The contestants and judges were standing there in the kitchen, the lights on the drum were flashing. They lit Patsy's face with a weird blue glow.

I wanted to shout, "HEY, SMUGFACE! Give my friend her recipe book back and admit what you have been up to!" But I knew that would give us away. And I suddenly felt nervous – this was our only chance to prove what had really been going on. What if it all went wrong?

smugface ALERT

"This is your last opportunity to prove to us you are a Bake or Break champion. Any one of you could blow us away with your final bake to win," said Harriet.

"Remember, Bake – don't Break!" said Spencer, as he turned the handle of the giant drum filled with mystery ingredients.

Patsy yawned. I couldn't believe she was so relaxed when she had done such horrible things. To my friend!

The contestants lined up to pick their mystery ingredient out of the drum.

"The drum!" I said, grabbing Poppy's hand and pulling her toward the kitchens. "It could already have been tampered with. Anything could be in there!"

the drum

Marie stepped toward the drum. I wanted to shout "Nooooooooo!" But we were too late. Marie reached inside.

I held my breath as Marie pulled out ... a box of Wheaty Wake-Up breakfast cereal. Phew.

"Agent Cupcake, people are looking at us," whispered Poppy. "Follow me."

Poppy started wiggling around and spelling out the letters of Bake or Break using her arms, like she'd done in the VIP area earlier. I tried to copy her, keeping an eye on what the contestants pulled out of the drum at the same time.

Primula got a packet of instant noodles and said, "WHAT am I supposed to do with this?"

Oliver looked relieved with his tin of mushy peas.

turnip

Violet got a turnip. Spencer Spokes gave her a thumbs-up. Violet didn't look happy.

Patsy stepped up last. She stuck her whole arm inside the drum and started pulling on something, as if it was stuck. Weird. She seemed to know exactly what she was looking for inside. She struggled for a while, then gave a massive tug, and pulled out – a bottle of maple syrup.

Hang on! I thought. Maple syrup is the main ingredient in the tastiest recipe in Grandma Maple's missing recipe book: THE MAPLE MARVEL. The very same recipe Violet had wanted to bake in the Show-Stopper Challenge!

11:00 AM
BAKE OR BREAK TENT, PATSY'S
KITCHEN AREA

The contestants were allowed a selection of extra ingredients from the store cabinet. Patsy strolled over and picked up four apples.

"OH NO, I'VE DROPPED SOME SUGAR!" Violet said loudly, bending down to pick up some sugar (that she hadn't really spilled).

This was the signal we had arranged earlier. It means: Mystery Girl Meeting Needed. Violet's worst fears were coming true. Patsy was going to try to win the competition with Grandma Maple's most special recipe and pretend it was HERS.

Poppy led the way to Violet, dancing and waving her arms. (I had to keep remembering that we were dressed as giant cakes and that this was the type of thing a giant cake mascot would do.)

"Patsy has maple syrup and now apples," whispered Violet. "She's baking MY grandma's secret recipe! It's her — Patsy is the cake saboteur."

"Don't worry, Violet, we're already onto her," said Poppy.

"I'm going to get a closer look. I bet she's got your grandma's recipe book in her cabinet," I said.

"Be careful!" said Violet.

Next time Patsy opens that cabinet, I'll be waiting. There's NO WAY she's going to get away with this.

apples + maple syrup = MAPLE MARVEL!

I darted behind Patsy when she opened her cabinet, trying to catch a glimpse of the recipe book I knew she was hiding in there. She turned and gave me one of her Ice Queen glares.

"Out of my way, cupcake!" she said, shoving me to one side.

I slipped ... and then it all happened too quickly for me to stop it. The cupcake icing hood of my costume slipped back over my head. My cover was blown.

"YOU!" Patsy said.

"IT'S THE CHEAT –
THE CHEAT IS BACK
IN THE BUILDING!"
yelled Primula.

my cover being BLOWN

The audience gasped.

Disaster! I didn't have any concrete evidence or conclusive proof yet. But now I just had to hope people would listen when I told them the truth.

"It's not me who is the cheat," I shouted. "The Mystery Girls have been framed by Patsy and her mom, Valerie Éclair!"

The audience gasped, again.

"I don't know WHAT you are talking about," said Patsy, folding her arms. Then she whispered, "Try proving it, cupcake!"

"I HAVE PROOF!" I shouted, flinging open Patsy's cabinet doors where I suspected Patsy was keeping Grandma Maple's recipe book. "In here is the recipe book Patsy and her mom stole from my friend, Violet Maple."

Poppy, still in her full donut costume, shouted, "Yeah, Patsy – you've been exposed!"

I looked in the cabinet.

Oh no.

Eggs, sugar, flour, baking powder. There was no book.

no recipe book!

"THIS IS OUTRAGEOUS!
How dare you accuse my
daughter of cheating?"
shouted Valerie Éclair.
She had stood up
and was clutching
her handbag.

SCARY!

"This really is unacceptable. You can't just go
around accusing contestants of cheating!" said
Harriet Blythington.

"And YOU are banned from Bake or Break!"
Spencer Spokes shouted at me.

"YOU HAVE NO PROOF!" screamed Valerie.
As she spoke, she pointed wildly. Valerie Éclair
looked scary. She had that same crazed look in
her eyes she'd had in that photograph from all
those years ago.

"You are just jealous of Patsy's baking talent!"
Valerie screamed, waving her arms.

Her handbag flew out of her grasp and landed on
the floor, the contents spilling everywhere.

Red lipstick,

a purse,

AND...

Grandma Maple's recipe book.

"That's MY grandma's recipe
book!" shouted Violet. I've never
seen her look so furious.

Harriet Blythington picked up the book and
an old photograph fluttered from the pages.
I grabbed it. This was the concrete evidence I'd
been hoping for!

In my hands was the same photograph I'd seen in Arthur's Bake or Break Annual – the winner from the year of "the scandal," the year Valerie Boggins was disqualified for cheating.

But on this photo, the head of Patsy Éclair had been cut out and stuck over the top of the winner's face. Patsy and Valerie are officially CRAZY!

"I think this is all the proof we need," I said, showing the photo to one of the camera crew. It appeared on the big screen. (I did my best serious detective face. It was great to get a chance to use it.) "This shows just how desperate Valerie Éclair is for her daughter to win Bake or Break."

I expected the audience to look more convinced, but they were all just sitting there, staring at me.

"Valerie and Patsy Éclair have been trying to ruin the other contestants' chances all the way through the competition," I said.

"First, Violet's recipe book mysteriously vanished, then the cupcakes were sabotaged. Oliver's incinerated volcano cupcakes and Primula's flat cupcakes were NO accident. Neither were the hairs in Marie's cupcakes ..."

Oliver gawked at me. Primula stared at Patsy. The audience seemed to be more convinced now, so I carried on. "It doesn't stop there. There was no freak gust of wind! Valerie Éclair pushed over the pies!"

"LIES!" yelled Valerie.
She had gone bright red.

fuming

"WHATEVER, Mother.
I told you not to carry
around that stupid recipe
book in your handbag!"
Patsy screamed. "Now I'll
never win, and it's all your fault!"

This was great! The Éclairs had made
themselves look totally guilty – with a little help
from the Mystery Girls, of course.

STUNNED

"Wait one minute," said Harriet
Blythington.

For a horrible moment
I thought she was going to
say that cheating doesn't
happen on Bake or Break.
But she was staring at the
photograph with Patsy's
head stuck on.

"Yes, Harriet," I said, realizing what she had finally understood. "Valerie Éclair used to be Valerie Boggins. She is the same Valerie who was disqualified from Bake or Break for cheating in the Year of the Scandal!"

The audience gasped again (for about the millionth time today).

"You two," Harriet said, staring at Valerie and Patsy, "are banned from Bake or Break. FOREVER."

I kind of wished I was wearing some sort of cool detective outfit instead of a giant cupcake costume – but it was still the most wonderful moment ever!

case
solved

And that wasn't even the best part. I looked at Violet and she was grinning. She was hugging Grandma Maple's recipe book to her chest, and that made all the stress worthwhile – we said we were going to get that book back for Violet, and we did.

Violet and the recipe book

What can I say? Solving this mystery was a piece of cake (honest)!

Piece of cake!

Friday
May 16th

NO MORE BAKE
OR BREAK!

WHAT'S NEXT FOR
THE MYSTERY GIRLS?

Some Maple
Marvel cake batter!

12:06 PM
MYSTERY GIRLS HQ, BEANBAG AREA

Things went a bit crazy after we revealed what
Patsy and her mom were up to. Marie got
really annoyed and shouted, "YOU RUINED MY
LEMON MERINGUE!" and threw cake mixture
at Patsy.

Primula made sure she was being filmed before
she flung her packet of instant noodles at Patsy's
head and shouted, "I knew it was you! I knew
all along!" (As if!) Oliver looked around to see if
he really should be doing this, then he started
flicking mushy peas at Patsy and her mom.

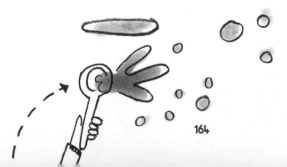

First it was just the contestants throwing food, then the audience joined in, too. It was totally insane! Valerie and Patsy were escorted from the Bake or Break tent covered in gunk – ha!

Ha!

It took the TV crew a while to tidy up the kitchen area after the food fight, but Harriet Blythington said she refused to let the competition end without a winner. The Drum Challenge was abandoned and the Show-Stopper Challenge was back on. Harriet said the competition was wide open and anyone could win.

Oliver used the mushy peas (the ones he didn't throw in the food fight) to make fish finger and mushy pea flavored mini ice cream cakes, which looked like real ice creams with chocolate stuck in them and everything.

← fish finger flavored

mushy pea

sticky toffee

Marie baked a giant sticky toffee pudding and there was so much that the audience got to taste some afterwards.

Primula opted for a cake shaped like a pony covered in pink icing and glitter. And Violet baked the Maple Marvel.

Now that she had the recipe book, Violet looked completely relaxed. She remembered all the complicated mixing techniques and new ingredients she had planned to add to her version of the Maple Marvel, without even really looking at her notes.

pony cake

The end result was
amazing – a three-
tiered Maple Marvel,
covered in creamy,
shimmery glitter icing
and little question
mark shaped apple
flavored truffles. YUM!

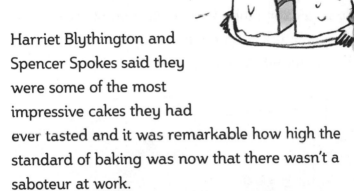

Harriet Blythington and
Spencer Spokes said they
were some of the most
impressive cakes they had
ever tasted and it was remarkable how high the
standard of baking was now that there wasn't a
saboteur at work.

In the end, Oliver took first prize. The judges said
his cakes were totally unique and different. Oliver
actually hugged Mr. Bunsworth when he found
out, which is a bit wimpy, but I suppose he was
just really happy. I could kind of see what they
meant about his cakes, but I'd rather eat Violet's
baking any day!

Violet came second and Marie got third place. (Primula wasn't happy about this, but the head of her pony cake was definitely wonky.)

Second place is wonderful but, even better, the judges said they thought the Mystery Maple Marvel had the potential to be as famous as one of Grandma Maple's recipes. WOW!

Bake or Break winners!

3:30 PM
MYSTERY GIRLS HQ, THE MYSTERY DESK

All of Puddleford is talking about Nightmare
Éclairs (that's what Patsy and her mom are
being called now) and how fantastic it is that the
Mystery Girls stopped them. We've had lots
of people asking us how we did it. It's been great
saying, "It was very simple in the end. There's
no mystery too mysterious and no problem too
perplexing for us!"

Violet has just been over with what was left
of her Maple Marvel cake. I've been eating it
while writing down everything that's happened
(mmmmmmm). Here is my case report in full:

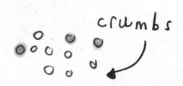

crumbs

THE CUPCAKE CONUNDRUM
SOLVED BY THE MYSTERY GIRLS (AVAILABLE
FOR ALL YOUR MYSTERY-SOLVING NEEDS)

This year's Junior Bake or Break competition fell victim to ruthless cake saboteurs in the form of finalist Patsy and Valerie Éclair. Valerie was desperate to ensure her daughter, Patsy, won the competition.

Valerie Éclair used to be Valerie Boggins, who got kicked out of the competition for cheating twenty-five years ago. She married a French bakery owner called Philippe Éclair and that's why nobody realized sooner that they were the same person.

MOTHER AND DAUGHTER IN CHEATING SCANDAL

SHOCKING ACTS OF SABOTAGE COMMITTED BY THE NIGHTMARE ÉCLAIRS:

1. They knew how famous Grandma Maple was for her delicious baked goods so they stole Grandma Maple's recipe book from her granddaughter, Violet Maple (Mystery Girl).

2. They sabotaged contestants' cupcakes by tampering with oven temperatures and adding hair to cake mixtures. (We haven't worked out how they made Primula's cakes flat.)

3. Valerie Éclair destroyed two of the contestants' lemon meringue pies. She had intended to destroy all the pies except Patsy's, but was disturbed by Charlotte Gordon (who was inside one of the pies).

4. Valerie Éclair planted a bag of evidence in Violet's cabinet to make it look as if she was the one trying to sabotage the competition.

smoke machine

5. Seeing that the bag of evidence had been removed by the Mystery Girls, Valerie decided to frame us as saboteurs instead. It is suspected that she tampered with a smoke machine backstage and filled the tent with thick black smoke.

6. The Éclairs picked the most famous recipe from Grandma Maple's recipe book for the final Drum Challenge, the Maple Marvel. Valerie Éclair made sure that Patsy got the right ingredients to bake this cake by taping a bottle of maple syrup to the inside of the drum. (We also suspect that she somehow ensured the other contestants received extremely challenging ingredients that were almost impossible to bake a cake with.)

tape

breakfast cereal

turnip

noodles

mushy peas

They almost got away with it, but thankfully the Nightmare Éclairs were brought to justice when Grandma Maple's recipe book was located inside Valerie Éclair's handbag. (Ha!)

valerie's handbag

It turns out Patsy hadn't even baked her own cake in the Children's Party Challenge! Valerie Éclair had brought an Eiffel Tower-shaped cake from her fancy bakery and switched it when the kitchens were evacuated. (The empty box was discovered in the backstage area.)

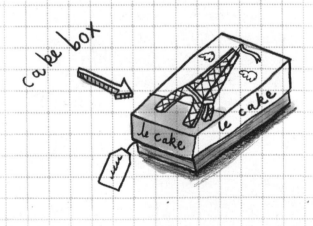

cake box

le cake   le cake

Violet has returned Grandma Maple's recipe book to her. Grandma Maple is so impressed by the new recipes Violet has added, she decided they should run a booth together at the Puddleford Village Festival in a few weeks. They are already getting loads of orders for Mystery Maple Marvels!

CASE CLOSED.

NOTE: If you require the services of the Mystery Girls, please get in touch very soon. We expect to be inundated with complex and mysterious mysteries to solve when Bake or Break is shown on TV in a few weeks' time, and may be extremely busy for a while.

Violet and Grandma
Maple